PARROTS
&
PIRATES

PARROTS & PIRATES

A Mystery at Sea

ELIZABETH LEVY

ILLUSTRATED BY MORDICAI GERSTEIN

ROARING BROOK PRESS

NEW YORK

Published by Roaring Brook Press
Roaring Brook Press is a division of Holtzbrinck Publishing Holdings
Limited Partnership
175 Fifth Avenue, New York, New York 10010
mackids.com

Library of Congress Cataloging-in-Publication Data

Levy, Elizabeth, 1942–
    Parrots & pirates : a mystery at sea / Elizabeth Levy ; illustrated by Mordicai Gerstein.
        p. cm.
    Summary: On board a cruise ship to Parrot Island, eleven-year-old Philippa Bath
suspects a new on-board entertainer of plotting to steal rare parrots.
    ISBN 978-1-59643-463-9
    [1. Cruise ships—Fiction.   2. Parrots—Fiction.   3. Crime—Fiction.   4. Mystery
and detective stories.]   I. Gerstein, Mordicai, ill.   II. Title.   III.
Title: Parrots and pirates.

PZ7.L5827Par   2011
[Fic]—dc22

                                                                      2010053003

Roaring Brook Press books are available for special promotions
and premiums.
For details contact: Director of Special Markets, Holtzbrinck Publishers.

First edition 2011
Book design by Scott Myles
Printed in October 2011 in the United States of America by
RR Donnelley & Sons Company, Harrisonburg, Virginia

1   3   5   7   9   8   6   4   2

To Mordicai Gerstein, with
love for all the years and all
the characters we share . . .

And to Nancy Mercado,
First Mate extraordinaire . . .
—E. L.

For two extraordinary friends:
Juliet and Tess
—M. G.

TABLE OF CONTENTS

PARROTS
&
PIRATES

CHAPTER ONE
"SECRETS!" SQUAWKED THE PARROT

"Excuse me, Don Quixote," I said. I stuck my hand into his cage. Feathers were everywhere. I couldn't believe how messy a parrot's cage could get. Don Quixote bent his majestic head with his curved beak toward me. He followed my every move, but he didn't attack me.

"You know Philippa, you're the only one he lets clean his cage, except me," said Philip.

We were in the captain's quarters, and I was helping Philip clean the cage for his parrot. Let me get something straight. I am *not* Philip's maid, even if he is the captain's son *and* the royal prince of Borgunlund. But

Philip is my best friend, and he has been in a lousy mood—no make that a black mood—ever since we set sail for Parrot Island. So I didn't mind helping him out—especially since I hoped it would give us a chance to talk. A ship isn't a great place for privacy.

"Philip, what's going on?" I asked. "I can tell that you've been upset since the beginning of this cruise."

Philip took a deep breath. He finally looked at me. "How did you know that I was upset?" he asked.

"It wasn't hard," I said.

Philip turned to me. "You know, I'm not used to having a friend who can read my moods. Only my mother used to be able to guess what I was feeling."

"You just haven't seemed your old self," I said to him.

"You're right," said Philip. "You know that Parrot Island used to belong to Borgunlund, but what you don't know is that my mother drowned just off Parrot Island," he said.

"I'm so sorry," I said. "I didn't know that's where she died."

"Don Quixote was with her," said Philip. He reached

into the cage, and Don Quixote stepped delicately onto his arm, the way he had been trained. I cleaned the bottom of the cage while Philip stroked his parrot. His voice was soft. "Don Q was a gift to my mother from Parrot Island when she was just my age. Parrots can live a long time, some get to be one hundred. Don Quixote is almost forty years old, and he's still young in parrot years. They are also very loyal. It means a lot to me that Don Quixote trusts you."

I smiled at Don Quixote. "You look very young for your age," I said to him. Don Quixote bobbed his head as if he agreed with me. "Fill up a bath!" he squawked. My last name is Bath. If you say my name fast enough it sounds like 'fill up a bath.' It's even funnier when a parrot squawks it.

"Don Quixote likes you," said Philip. "My mom would have been glad that you're coming with me to Parrot Island."

"I'm surprised your father and you even agreed to come back to Parrot Island," I said. "He's the captain. He could have refused to sail the ship there, or taken a short leave for this leg of the trip."

"Father *was* thinking of refusing but I want to see it again. I loved it there. My family used to vacation on Parrot Island together all the time. I'm kind of looking forward to going there with you."

Philip walked out onto his balcony. I closed Don Quixote's cage. I looked around Philip's and his father's stateroom. Everywhere you looked there was evidence of his mother's love of parrots. Besides Don Quixote, Philip had inherited his mother's magnificent collection of mechanical parrots.

I joined Philip on the balcony. Only the captain and his family get a suite of rooms with a balcony. My parents work on the ship, too—Mom's a dancer, Dad teaches water sports and karate—but we live below the waterline in a room without a porthole. Still, I love life on board and wouldn't want to live anywhere else. But it was a lot more fun when Philip wasn't so sad.

Philip was staring out at sea. I could see the lights of a small pilot ship, the kind that guide big ships like ours in and out of harbors. It was heading for us.

"Can I tell you a secret?" asked Philip. His voice

sounded lighter. Maybe just talking about his mother had eased his mind a little.

"Does anybody ever answer 'no'?" I teased him. "Who doesn't want to know a secret?"

Philip pointed to the pilot boat coming toward us. "There's the secret. We're getting a new assistant cruise director and they sent a special pilot boat with him. Somebody high up in the cruise line insisted he be hired."

This wasn't normal! Usually, the only time the cruise ship would let someone board like this was if they were a VIP, or some celebrity that had missed the sailing deadline. I couldn't remember them ever sending a pilot ship for a new crewmember before.

A ladder was lowered to the pilot ship. A man jumped onto the ladder. He was very agile.

Then something even stranger happened. The man gestured to the crew to lower a hoist, and he pointed to an old trunk!

"That's weird," I said to Philip. "What crewmember would come on late and bring a trunk?"

Philip shrugged. "It's just his luggage."

"Only a captain's son would say that," I said to Philip. "You've seen the room my parents and I live in. A cockroach in a roach motel has more room! Nobody who works on a cruise ship ever comes with a lot of luggage. There's something weird about this dude. Let's go meet him. A mystery may be just what you and I need."

Philip grinned at me. "It's you who can't resist a mystery," he said.

"It's both of us," I said.

We walked back into Philip's cabin. "See you later, Don Quixote," I said as we passed the parrot's cage.

"In a while crocodile," squawked Don Quixote. I laughed. "I taught him that," I said proudly.

"I taught him a new word too," said Philip. " Secrets," said Philip.

"Secrets!" squawked Don Quixote.

"Why did you teach him to say that?" I asked Philip.

"Because I knew you loved secrets," said Philip. "Even though I was in a bad mood, I wanted to have a surprise for you."

I smiled. Sometimes Philip really did surprise me.

"Okay," I said to Don Quixote. "We're going to find out the secret behind that guy with the huge trunk..."

Don Quixote cocked his head and looked back at me.

"Secrets!" he squawked again.

CHAPTER TWO
A LITTLE BUZZ

Philip and I ran down the steps to the lower deck. It was much quicker than waiting for the elevator. It always amazes us how passengers will wait for the elevator for the longest time, just to avoid even one flight of steps.

Captain Vittiganen smiled at me and waved us over. I know he likes that Philip and I have become good friends. I have a feeling that Philip led a pretty lonely life before his father and he came onto the S.S. *Excalibur*. Philip has had a tough life, even if he was brought up as a little royal prince.

Camilla was standing next to the captain, and she didn't look at all pleased to see me. In fact, she looked as if she had swallowed something sour. But that wasn't too surprising. Camilla Trout was our cruise director, and she almost always looked as if she were sucking on a lemon.

"Philippa," said the captain. "Come meet our new assistant cruise director, Herbert Twining."

"Call me Herby." The guy stuck his hand out to me.

I instantly got a tickling sensation in my palm. It didn't hurt, but it sure felt funny!

I jumped back. Herby opened his palm and showed me the buzzer that was in it.

Then he held his hand out to Philip. I wasn't sure that was such a good idea. After all, Philip was the captain's son and this guy was supposed to be part of the crew. Everybody on ship, including me, was careful around the captain. "So you're the captain's son," said Herby.

Philip took his hand. Philip had been taught as a royal prince to shake hands firmly, do a little bow, and almost click his heels.

Philip grasped Herby's hand firmly in his. The buzz was so loud that Camilla jumped even farther back from Philip.

"Whoo-hoo!" said Herby.

Philip started to look offended, but then he began to laugh. "How did you do that?" he asked.

"How dare you play a practical joke on the captain's son, of all people!" said Camilla.

I noticed that Camilla didn't seem to care that Herby had also pulled the joke on me. But I was used to not counting in Camilla's world. She was the boss of my parents, and she considered herself the boss of me, too.

Just then Camilla's daughters, the Trout twins, Ruby and Sapphire, came up to us. They are just two years younger than Philip and me. Philip and I are almost twelve. When Philip first came on board the twins thought that Philip would be *their* friend—not mine, since technically Camilla ranks higher than my parents. The twins can sometimes be as snobby and snotty as their mother.

Philip grinned at Herby. "Give them the buzz!" he whispered.

Herby held his hand out to Ruby. She screamed as if she had been electrocuted! Camilla snatched the buzzer out of Herby's hand before he could do it to Sapphire.

"Mommy! He gave me a shock!" screamed Ruby.

"A shock!" repeated Sapphire, even though she hadn't been touched. The twins have an annoying habit of repeating each other.

"Enough!" shouted Camilla. "I will not allow this kind of foolishness on my ship."

Herby winked at Philip. I didn't get this guy. First, he played a practical joke on the captain's son, and then on his boss's kids. It was the kind of thing that could get him kicked off the ship before he even started his job.

But, to my surprise, the captain defended him. Captain Vittiganen coughed. "Technically, Camilla, it is my ship, and I don't think anybody was harmed by his little joke. Perhaps you will show Mr. Twining to his quarters."

"Somebody else can lead him to his room," snapped Camilla. "I have too much to do. Philippa's mother has a new pirate and parrot-themed show planned, and I

have to make sure of the details. Although I have to admit that if it works it will be quite spectacular."

Leave it to Camilla to give a backhanded compliment—my mom taught me that term. By saying that big word "IF" Camilla made it sound as if she didn't think Mom's show would work. But I knew it would and I felt proud. I knew all about Mom's parrot and pirate extravaganza, and it was going to be great.

"We'll take him to his room," I said quickly. Herby clapped one hand on my shoulder and one on Philip's. "Lead on! Take me to my room. I can't wait to open the porthole and smell those sea breezes."

I stared at him.

"Is anything wrong?" he asked me.

"Have you ever worked on a ship before?" I asked him.

"Oh, sure," said Herby breezily. "Lots of experience. Whoo-hoo!"

CHAPTER THREE

A ROYAL PAIN

We took the elevator below decks. "Hey," said Herby, dragging his trunk behind him. "Are you sure you know where you're taking me? This looks awfully different from the rest of the cruise ship."

"Welcome to our world," I said.

Herby's trunk noisily rolled along on the metal floors. Where we live there is no carpeting on the floor. The shiny metal walls are bare, except for a few posters from around the world taped to the walls. It's completely different from the rich colors and expensive materials that greet passengers in their hallways.

Philip let me lead the way—we were on my turf now. It was like a maze down in the quarters where my parents and I and most of the crew sleep. Herby was having trouble maneuvering the chest as we walked through the narrow corridors.

We ran into my mother, and I introduced her to Herby. Mom was dressed in a feathered costume, one that the costume department had designed for the parrot and pirate extravaganza.

She starred at Herby's trunk. "What do you have in there?" she asked.

"Oh, there's magic in this chest. That's why it always comes with me. May I say that you look like quite a rare bird in that costume?"

Mom laughed and patted her feathers. "I'm rehearsing for a new show we are putting on to celebrate the parrots of Parrot Island. I see you've already met my daughter, Philippa."

"I met her, but I didn't know her last name was Bath. Fill up a bath!" chortled Herby. He didn't sound as cute as Don Quixote.

Mom winked at me. "I know," she said. "But *Philippa*

means 'lover of horses,' and she loves all animals. Both her father and I loved the name."

"My name means 'lover of horses,' too," said Philip. "It was the first thing I felt I had in common with Philippa when I came onto this ship." He grinned at me. Whoever Herby was, I had to give him credit. He definitely seemed to have brought Philip out of his funk. "Are you in charge of entertainment?" Herby asked Mom.

"Yes, it's very exciting. I've choreographed a whole new routine for my dance crew, and we've got pirate and parrot events planned for the whole week. You picked a busy week to join us."

Herby's eyes gleamed. "Maybe I can help. I'm a bit of an amateur magician, you know."

"Thanks," said Mom. "But, you'll have your hands full being Camilla's assistant."

I knew Mom was being nice. The truth was that Camilla was not at all easy to work with. "Welcome aboard," Mom said cheerfully. "I've got to go, and you should get settled. Camilla runs a tight ship."

Mom went off, and we walked down one of the

corridors toward the back of the ship. Camilla had managed to give Herby one of the worst rooms, right between the engine and the crew rec room with its Ping-Pong table.

My dad was playing Ping-Pong with one of the chefs from Indonesia. I waved to them, and then introduced them to Herby.

Herby stuck out his hand. Dad jumped back when he got the buzzer in Herby's hand. I should have warned him.

"I can see you're going to add some buzz to this cruise," Dad said with a laugh. He introduced Herby to Chef Do. "My hands are my fortune," said the chef, smiling. "No buzzing…"

"I wouldn't want to hurt the hand that's going to feed me," said Herby.

"Anyhow," said Chef Do, "I must go. It's time for my shift." He put down his paddle.

"Care for a game?" Herby said casually to Dad.

"Don't you want to get settled first?" asked Dad.

"Oh, just one friendly game," said Herby. "I don't play much."

Herby began to stretch. Then he reached into his backpack and brought out his own paddle. Dad and I glanced at each other. Not many people carry around their own Ping-Pong paddle.

"Are you sure you don't play much?" asked Dad. Herby served. The ball zipped past my father with a dangerous topspin.

"He's good," Philip whispered to me.

Dad's eyes narrowed. He got his game face on. My dad hates to lose.

Herby unleashed another serve. This time, Dad put him away with a sharp forehand.

"Go, Dad!" I shouted.

Herby aced his serve. Philip clapped for him. I glared at Philip.

"What?" asked Philip. "I know you want your dad to win, but Herby's good, too."

The game seesawed back and forth. Soon the rec room was crowded with crewmembers cheering for Dad. In the end he beat Herby, 11–9. Dad put down his paddle and shook Herby's hand.

"I guess I met my match," said Herby.

"Herby's a good sport," said Philip admiringly.

I bit my lip. "Yeah, but he lied about not playing much," I whispered back.

Dad clapped his hands together. "Welcome aboard. I've got to go. The weather report isn't good, and I have to make some alternate plans for the guests in case we have to close the swimming pool."

"I'd better unpack and see what Camilla has in store for me," said Herby. We took Herby to his room. I kind of hoped that Herby would show us what was in the trunk, but he made it clear that he wanted to be alone. "Thanks, kids," he said.

Philip and I took the staircase back to the deck. I couldn't wait to talk to Philip. We both loved mysteries and Herby was one gift-wrapped mystery! "Herby said he's worked on cruise ships before," I said urgently when we were alone. "But he didn't know that his room wouldn't have a porthole, and he didn't know what the crew's quarters looked like. He thought that my mom might actually need an amateur's help. And what about that trunk? There's got to be something suspicious in it. I think we should try to get a look inside when he's not around."

Philip looked offended. "That would not be nice," he said in his most royal voice. "Besides, Herby is very funny ... he's like a court jester."

Philip had been in a royal court, and I guess the court jesters all worked for the royal family. Philip never had to worry. He and his father were at the top of the totem pole.

Having a joker in the pack was fun—but not if he was your parents' boss—and technically Herby rated above my parents. It could mean trouble.

CHAPTER FOUR

A JOKE IN BAD TASTE

The next morning, I could feel a change in the atmosphere. Passengers hate when their vacations are ruined by a storm. But the sea is a funny creature, and we really can't control her. If you get to know the seas as well as I do, you can read her moods. The waters looked calm, but it was difficult to see where the sky and water met. They were both overlapping in grays, which meant that a storm was coming soon—maybe not right away, but it was definitely on the horizon.

Passengers come on our cruises to escape from their

normal lives—and that's what we like to give them. We don't want them to have any stress—just fun. However, it's not always as easy as it seems to make a voyage stress-free.

Philip and I went up to the kennels. The kennels are mostly for passengers who pay to bring their pets on board. As the captain's son, Philip not only gets to keep his parrot, but also his big, royal, standard poodle, Max. Until Philip, I had never been allowed to have a pet. Then a few months ago, I got to keep Lady Windermere, a little Havapoo that a passenger smuggled on board and then abandoned.

Lady Windermere's tail is covered in so much hair that her whole backside goes into motion when she's wagging her tail. Max, as always, looked more dignified. Philip and I snapped on their leashes.

"It smells like a storm," I said to Philip.

"You're right," said Philip. "My father is worried. There *is* a big storm off the coast of Africa, and we may have to take the ship slightly off course to avoid the rough seas."

"At least the passengers will have a lot to distract

them," I said. Even Camilla said that pirates and parrots is a winner for this week's theme!"

"Isn't it only in those American cartoons and movies that pirates go with parrots?" asked Philip.

"You are so wrong," I told Philip. "Pirates and parrots isn't just some cartoon joke. Pirates really did capture parrots and bring them back to sell for a fortune. And did you know that there were a lot of famous women pirates? Women pirates were some of the best-known pirates in the world. One of them even met Queen Elizabeth."

"I met Queen Elizabeth the second once," said Philip. "She was very nice. She likes dogs."

"I still can't get used to the fact that I am actually friends with someone who can say 'Oh, yes, I know the Queen of England.'"

"Well, Queen Elizabeth looked normal compared to some of our passengers," said Philip. "I can't believe that some of them are already dressed up as pirates."

It was true. A few of our passengers had already gotten into the spirit of things by wearing pirate hats, pirate patches, and big blousy "pirate" pants. There even were glittering pirate shirts with skulls and cross-bones. It's not just kids who would like to dress up; on cruises, it's the adults who really love wearing costumes.

"Whoo-hoo!" shouted Herby, coming up to us. He was also wearing a puffy pirate shirt. Lady Windermere's little bottom began wagging back and forth. Max as always was a little more dignified.

"Are you walking one of the passenger's dogs?" Herby asked me.

"No," I said. "She's mine."

Herby raised one eyebrow. I always wondered how people could do that. When I try to raise one eyebrow, my whole forehead moves like a weird cartoon.

"I'm surprised that they let *you* have a pet on board."

"Your right," I admitted. "She's a stray who was abandoned on board . . . and since Philip already had two pets—his parrot and his poodle, I got to keep her."

"Only because she's friends with Philip," said Ruby, coming up to us. I hadn't realized that they were listening to us. The twins were each wearing big, puffy white shirts and pirate hats.

Just then a lady with a feather boa turned around. She was wearing a pirate hat, a spyglass, and huge binoculars hung around her neck. "What a cute dog!" she said. Her feathers drooped as she bent down to pet Lady Windermere. The binoculars and boa around her neck got tangled up with the leash. Her spyglass bopped Lady Windermere on the head.

"Let me help you," said Philip. Together, Philip and I got the lady and her boa and binoculars untangled from poor Lady Windermere's leash.

"Thank you," she said. "I'm Mrs. Totaa."

The lady stood up and flung her boa back around her neck. She waved to a passenger coming towards us. "Yoo-hoo! Mr. Papegeno!"

The man waved back. He was pulling a big rolling suitcase. The suitcase was almost as big as Herby's trunk. It seemed to be made out of fake snakeskin. At least I hoped it was fake. I hated to think about how many real snakes would have had to die to make that suitcase. I don't love snakes, but I don't think they should be used for luggage. The man was also wearing a pirate hat with a green feather on it. Around his neck he wore a necklace with snakeskin with a sharp tooth hanging from it.

"Hello, there Mr. Papageno. I was just admiring this little dog. I heard that the captain has a dog. Young lady, is this the captain's little dog?"

Max was more than six feet tall when he stood on his hind legs. Nobody would ever call Max "little."

"Oh," trilled the woman. "I just met Mr. Papageno and he tells me that he's a painter. Mr. Papageno, isn't that wonderful? You should paint these adorable dogs."

Mr. Papegeno smiled at us. "I came on this journey mostly to paint birds, but I'm an artist who loves to paint all animals. I've got my easels and paint in this suitcase."

Mr. Papegeno turned his attention away from Philip toward me. "I see you're admiring my rattlesnake tooth," he said. "It comes from a rattlesnake that I caught on one of my journeys."

I didn't know how to tell the man that I wasn't admiring it. It creeped me out.

"Actually, sir, Philippa really doesn't like snakes," said Philip.

"Doesn't like snakes," said Ruby.

"Hates snakes," said Sapphire.

I felt I had to say something. "I know snakes are often good for the environment, and some people find them beautiful..." I stammered.

"Admit it," said Philip to me. "You hate snakes."

"Hate snakes," I admitted.

"What do you get when you cross a snake and a Lego set?" asked Herby.

"I don't know," I admitted.

"A boa constructor!" Herby laughed as if it was a great joke, and so did Ruby and Sapphire. Even Philip was giggling. Mr. Papageno let go of his suitcase to give Herby a high five. The ship rolled, and the suitcase started to roll with it.

I grabbed it.

Herby didn't even notice. What was with this guy! Anybody who worked on a ship before would have helped the passenger out. That's our job.

"Excuse me, sir," I said to the man, trying not to look

at his rattlesnake tooth. "Would you like me to get a steward to take that suitcase to your cabin?" I knew I was being a little prissy. I wanted Herby to know that was one of the things that *he* should be doing.

Herby wasn't paying any attention. "Are you a bird-watcher?" he asked Mrs. Totaa. "I'm a rare bird," said Herby. I am a comedi-HEN!"

Mrs. Totaa laughed, and when she did her whole boa did a little dance.

"What's orange and sounds like a carrot?" asked Mrs. Totaa.

We stared at her. Her joke made no sense. "A carrot?" I asked.

Mrs. Totaa giggled. "I meant to say parrot... I'm not very good at jokes."

I tried to smile politely, but she was right. She wasn't good at telling jokes.

"I've got one for you folks," said Mr. Pappegno. "A young magician worked on a cruise ship, and he had a parrot, but the parrot would tell the audience how he did the trick, which as you know is a magic no-no. But one day the ship sank and the parrot and the magician

were alone on a lifeboat. Finally, the parrot squawked, "Okay, I give up. What did you do with the ship?"

Herby started laughing, and so did Ruby and Sapphire. But Philip became almost deathly quiet. I looked down at Max. He had sat back on his haunches, and he was emitting a very low growl. I had almost never heard Max growl.

Mr. Papageno noticed Philip's silence. "Oops," he said. "I guess, maybe it's not a good idea to tell a joke about sinking while you're on a cruise ship."

Herby looked at Philip. "Are you okay, son?" he asked.

"Yes, I am fine," said Philip, but I could tell from his voice that he wasn't.

"We have to finish walking our dogs," I said. I guided Philip to a quiet part of the deck. "Philip," I whispered, "what's wrong?"

Philip stared at me. "What do you mean?"

"One minute you were laughing at Herby and Mr. Papageno's jokes, the next minute you looked as if you wanted to shout, 'Off with their heads!' You know we often have to laugh at passengers' jokes or answer their stupid questions."

"I didn't like those two passengers. She even looks like a bird," said Philip. "No wonder she's named for a bird."

"Who?" I asked. "What bird?" I asked.

"*Totaa* means 'bird' in Hindi," said Philip.

"I can't believe you know Hindi," I said.

"My mother was interested in India," said Philip. "She wanted me to learn as many languages as I could..."

When he mentioned his mother, Philip looked angry again.

"Don't be angry at the passengers," I said to Philip. "They just want to laugh and have a good time."

We walked our dogs back to the kennel, around the port side of the ship, away from the sunset and the sunset bar—that's where there are always fewer passengers. Passengers always bunch around the places where there is free food and drinks.

Philip smiled at me. "I am not used to having a friend. My mother used to love to be alone. I am a little like her."

"Aren't you a little lonely when you are alone?"

"Most Americans seem to be with people all the

time, more than we are in Borgunlund. But I like being with you and other Americans—or at least *most* other Americans. I like Herby."

I looked out at the sea. The storm seemed to be moving closer.

CHAPTER FIVE
DOING THE TROUT

The dinner buffet was set out on the Palladium Deck. The buffets on our ship are like works of art in a museum. Our master chefs arrange and sculpt food into towering creations. The passengers stop and take pictures on their cell phones as if they were in front of a van Gogh painting. Vegetables are carved to look like flowers from the most exotic garden, and even some meats are formed into the shapes of houses, trains, and airplanes.

Philip and I were walking past the buffet when the Trout twins came up to us. "Your friend is supposed to do the dinner entertainment," said Sapphire, "but no-body can find him!"

"Yeah, nobody," repeated Ruby.

"My friend?" I asked her.

"That Herby guy," said Ruby. "Mom says that he is not going to last long. He's never where he's supposed to be."

"There he is now," said Philip, pointing to the bal-cony of the restaurant. Herby Twining was standing with a microphone in his hand.

Every night at the dinner service, the cruise staff and the waitstaff give the guests a little entertainment. It usually is a silly song or a dance. The guests always laugh seeing their waiter or dining room captain suddenly start singing "Under the Sea" from *The Little Mermaid* or doing the Macarena.

I wondered which song Herby was going to pick.

"Ladies and gentlemen, kids of all ages, may I hear a whoo-hoo?" Herby shouted into the microphone. "Whoo-hoo! I am happy to be among you. Tonight I want to teach you a new song. 'There is A TROUT TO BE TOUTED!'"

Almost everybody in the cruise industry knew that Camilla Trout did not have a sense of humor about herself. I looked across the room. Camilla's face had turned bright red. I once read in a book the expression "eyes shooting daggers" at a person. Until now it had always just seemed like an expression. Now it looked as if actual daggers were coming out of Camilla's eyes.

Herby pretended to swim around the room. Every time he passed a table, he got more people to follow him. As if by magic, he kept pulling out tiny bottles of bubbles and wands. He handed them out to all the children and to many of the grown-ups.

Soon the room was full of men, women, and kids, all blowing bubbles like a trout.

Herby taught them how to dance by stretching his arms out to the side, pretending to lead a school of fish through the dining room, with everyone shimmying their hips.

Philip grabbed my hand. We jumped in and started doing the Trout! I felt a hand on my shoulder. It was Mrs. Totaa. She looked even more like a bird than ever—a red cardinal. She had on a long red dress with

a red boa to match. She must have one for every occasion.

The other passengers were all flapping their arms. Across the room, I saw Mr. Papageno dancing and rolling his suitcase. He had even brought it to dinner. He looked as if he were having a great time.

Suddenly the music stopped abruptly. And so did Herby. Camilla grabbed Herby by the arm and hustled him out of the dining room. The captain followed.

"Come on," I said to Philip.

"Where are we going?" asked Philip.

"We want to find out what Herby is saying to Camilla and the captain," I said.

"Right," said Philip. "We don't want him to get fired."

I didn't have the nerve to tell Philip that I didn't feel as protective of Herby as he did.

Out in the corridor, Camilla was yelling at the captain and pointing to Herby. "Captain, as you know, Herbert Twining was not my hire. And as for this ridiculous dance..."

The captain put his finger up. "Enough!" he commanded. Camilla's mouth snapped shut. She did look a little like a trout. "You know that we never discuss internal ship's business in public areas," continued the captain. "Come with me to my quarters."

"Let's go," I said to Philip. "If we can get up to your quarters before them, maybe we can hear what's going on from your bedroom."

There is a secret maze behind the public corridors of the ship. These are the passages that the maids and stewards use to haul laundry and to clean the rooms.

We went through the maze of corridors and luckily got up to the top bridge before the captain. We went into Philip's quarters and hid in his room with the door open a crack so we could hear the captain, Herby, and Camilla as they entered the room.

"I know you have a lot on your mind, Captain," said Camilla. "But I cannot work with this new hire and his constant 'whoo-hoos.' I know that the cruise is worried about expenses and asking if we can make cutbacks." She was practically snorting. "I insist that he be the first one cut."

I took a sharp breath when I heard Camilla say that the cruise line wanted to make cutbacks. Our cruise line was special in that they let me live on board with my parents. What if one of the cutbacks was me! Philip, as the captain's son, would be allowed to live on board—and probably Camilla's girls, too. Maybe Herby had come on board to secretly find out how the cruise line could save money! Maybe that's why he was asking me about Lady Windermere.

Philip and I listened through the crack in the door to his bedroom.

"Camilla, I am going to have to overrule you on this," said the captain. "First of all, I have seen some of the passengers' comments. They are very favorable to Mr. Twining. Second, we are going to need everyone to pull together to keep our guests happy. The weather report is anything but promising for this cruise."

"May I say something, Captain?" said Herby. "I want to apologize to Camilla if she found my dance disrespectful. I had heard the weather reports, and I thought it would be good to have something cheerful to keep the passengers' minds off the weather."

"A very good point," said the captain.

Just then the ship rolled and the door to Philip's room flew open, revealing our hiding spot.

Herby saw us.

"What are you two doing eavesdropping?" Camilla demanded.

Philip put on his most royal prince look. "This is my stateroom," he said. "I was just showing Philippa some books I had in the closet . . . about Parrot Island."

As if on cue, Don Quixote suddenly squawked, "Fill up a bath!" I was grateful to the old bird. He distracted everyone.

"What a magnificent parrot," said Herby. He moved closer to Don Quixote's cage to get a better look.

Herby saw me staring at him. He studied me. His gaze was a little unnerving, like a parrot's. He made me nervous. "Do you like birds?" Herby asked.

"I like all animals—except snakes," I said, nervously. Even though I paid for Lady Windermere's dog food out of my allowance, I suddenly became very afraid that Herby was here to figure out where to make cuts— and where better than a little Havapoo—and me!

"This is a most interesting ship," said Herby. He turned to the captain. "I have a lot to think about before I write my report. Will you excuse me?"

The captain nodded.

"What report?" Camilla demanded.

Herby coughed. "Oh, I'm just writing a blog about working on a cruise ship," he said.

Camilla looked at him suspiciously. I was suspicious too.

"I'm scared," I whispered to Philip.

"What about?" Philip asked.

"Herby," I said.

"Oh," said Philip. "Don't worry. You heard what my father said. Herby will keep his job."

I swallowed hard. It wasn't Herby I was worried about, it was my parents' jobs and me. I decided to keep my worries to myself for a while. It was weird. Usually, it was Philip who kept things from me, but now it was me who was keeping things from Philip.

CHAPTER SIX
ROGUE WAVE

The next morning the ship was pitching and rolling. I heard my mother retching in the toilet. Mom loves living on a cruise ship, and we don't hit heavy weather often, but when it happens, it's always Mom who gets seasick. Everybody believes that seasick medicine can work wonders, but honestly, there is no magic to getting through a bout of seasickness. You just have to endure it.

"Is Mom okay?" I asked Dad.

Mom came out of the bathroom. Her legs were wobbly.

I got her a wet washcloth and put it on her forehead.

She gave me a sad smile, the one she always gives me when she gets seasick.

"It's not a picnic," said Mom. Dad grinned at her.

Dad always teases Mom about her sunny personality. She always thinks life is a picnic. So when she says, "It's not a picnic," I know that she really isn't feeling well.

"I'll be fine," said Mom, giving my hand a squeeze. "Go up and get some fresh air."

"Mom's right," said Dad. "Why don't you go up and walk Lady Windermere around the deck?"

As I was getting dressed, I heard Mom telling Dad that she was really worried about the big parrots and pirates extravaganza in the theater. "It's not just my being seasick," she said. "The cruise line put a lot of money into our pirate sets, but they won't work if the ship is pitching and rolling like this."

"Don't worry about tonight," my father said. "It'll all work out."

"Dad," I interrupted. "If the weather is so bad that Mom can't dance, and you can't do water sports . . . maybe that's not a good thing. Maybe the cruise line won't like it."

"Sweetheart, it's just a storm. It'll blow over soon.

Stop worrying. Now go get some fresh air and take Lady Windermere for a walk."

I went up on deck. But it wasn't easy to stop worrying. It's not as if there is a stop worrying button in my brain.

Lady Windermere looked happy to see me when I arrived at the kennel. But poor Max of Borgunlund didn't look so happy.

Philip joined me at the kennel. He seemed in an unusually good mood. He looked at me. "You look kind of glum," he said.

"My mom's seasick," I told him.

"Nobody in my family ever gets seasick." bragged Philip.

"You make it sound as if getting seasick is a weakness," I grumbled. "There's no reason to brag about never getting seasick." The wind had picked up, and I realized that I was yelling at Philip, perhaps a little louder than I should have.

"Are you okay?" Philip asked. "You aren't feeling seasick yourself, are you? I've never seen you like this."

"No, I'm not seasick," I said. "It's just that some very good sailors can get seasick, and it doesn't mean that they aren't as good a sailor as you. The Greeks wrote about getting seasick in the *Odyssey*. The guy who wrote that famous book about a whale, *Moby Dick*? He got seasick."

"You don't have to bite my nose off," said Philip. "You must have gotten up on the wrong side of the room this morning."

"It's the wrong side of the bed," I snapped at him. "Not the wrong side of the room! And it's bite your head off!"

I felt badly that I had corrected Philip. It wasn't a nice thing to do to someone. It's not as if I could speak as many languages as Philip did. Maybe I *had* gotten up on the wrong side of the bed.

"Well, whatever it is, I think today it is *you* who is in the bad mood" said Philip. He looked proud of himself. "See, I am a good friend, too. I can read your moods as well as you can read mine."

"Maybe you are right. This storm has made me edgy."

There were very few passengers out on the upper deck. Most were staying in their cabins to try to ride out the bad weather.

But Mr. Papageno was there with his art supplies, although it was too rocky to paint. "Ahoy!" he shouted to us. "This is some weather we're having."

Lady Windermere wagged her tail at him. Max didn't look as if he were at all in the mood to wag his tail.

"Maybe you should get one of these seasick patches like I'm wearing for that poodle! It's doing wonders for me. I feel in the pink!"

"My poodle is fine!" said Philip, almost as rudely as I had just spoken to him. Apparently he still hadn't forgiven Mr. Papageno for making that joke. But Mr. Papageno was a paying customer, and I didn't want him reporting back that the kids on the cruise were being rude.

I shot Philip a look. "We'll be out of the storm soon," I said.

"Good," said Mr. Papageno. "I am looking forward to the pirate extravaganza. I hope the crew doesn't have trouble performing on these high seas."

"There's nothing to worry about, sir," said Philip. "My father is setting a different course. We will avoid the storm."

"I hope that doesn't mean we'll avoid Parrot Island," said Mr. Papageno. He chuckled. "I'm so looking forward to seeing the rare birds."

"Don't worry," I said, hoping to reassure him. "This ship moves fast when we have to. The captain will be able to have us back on course as soon as the storm passes."

Mrs. Totaa came out on the deck. Mr. Pappegeno waved to her. Today she wasn't wearing a pirate outfit. She had on a pea green boa that matched her sickly green sweatpants and jacket. It was not a pretty outfit, and her complexion looked as green as her clothes.

"Are you feeling all right?" I asked her.

"Oh, oh . . . Well, no," moaned Mrs. Totaa sounding a little like a sick bird. "I do hope I am better by the time we get to Parrot Island. It's been my dream of a lifetime to see the parrots there." She belched.

"Fresh air is the best thing for you," said Mr. Papageno, cheerfully. "I'll accompany you on a promenade around the deck." He took Mrs. Totaa's hand.

"I don't really like that man," said Philip, watching them go.

"He was being very nice to Mrs. Totaa," I said. "This is a tough voyage. We should be doing everything we can to keep our passengers happy."

"Well," said Philip, brightening, "We *are* going to make

the passengers happy. I volunteered you! I have a huge surprise for you. Herby heard that your mother was seasick and was worried about canceling the show. He's going to put on a magic show and he thought you and I—and Don Quixote—would be the perfect assistants. I really think it will be fun. So I convinced father to let us do it. Isn't that great? We are going to be in a magic act!"

"But how did Herby find out so quickly that Mom was seasick?" I asked. "And she might get better. I don't like the idea that he's taking over Mom's show."

Philip stared at me. "He's not taking over your mother's show. He's helping out. My father said that he's a *go-getter*. Is that the correct English term?"

"It is," I admitted. "I'm just worried about exactly what it is that he wants to get."

"You have turned into a worrywart," said Philip.

I turned away from Philip and looked out at sea. When you're in the middle of the ocean, the waves can look deceptively small. But every once in a while, you get a rogue wave. They appear only in deep water. Our ship was big enough that we could take one of them in stride. But I felt like a rogue wave was on board.

CHAPTER SEVEN
WHOO-HOO YOURSELF

Right before our first rehearsal, Philip and I went to his quarters to get Don Quixote. Don Quixote's head was shaking from side to side. "Fill up a BATH!" he squawked when he saw me.

"He looks nervous," I said to Philip.

"No," said Philip. "When he waves his head like that, it just means that he wants attention. He's a ham."

Philip lifted Don Quixote and his cage from its stand. We took the elevator to the theater level. The passengers all stared at us. Don Quixote kept nodding his head as if he were a king greeting his subjects.

We entered the theater from backstage. Our theater is designed to dazzle from the front, but from the back it is a mess.

All the backstage sets are hung from the ceiling and lowered by ropes and pulleys. It is far less glamorous on this side of the curtain than when you're sitting in the audience.

As soon as I stepped onto the stage I could feel the dance floor dipping with the rolling of the ship. When the dance floor pitches, it gets dangerous to move the elaborate stage sets.

Herby was standing in the middle of the stage as if he were the ringmaster and this was his circus. Ruby and Sapphire came up to us. "Herby is going to put on a magic show," said Ruby.

"Real magic," said Sapphire.

"With jokes," said Ruby.

"Lots of jokes," said Sapphire.

"I thought you didn't like him," I said. "You got mad when he buzzed you."

"Oh, Mom said that he's a real go-getter," said Ruby.

"Go-getter," repeated Sapphire.

Philip winked at me. "It was the right word," he whispered.

I nodded, but I was worried.

If Camilla was now being nice to Herby, maybe it meant that she had found out that the 'report' he was doing was to make cuts for the cruise line. Now she wanted to stay on the good side of him.

Mom was standing in the wings in her parrot costume. She had managed to get out of bed. Unfortunately, she looked as green as the color of the feathers on her costume.

I went over to her, but before I could ask her how she was feeling, Herby came to us and said to my mom, "You look lovely as a parrot. But I know you aren't feeling well enough to dance. The show will go on! Why don't you go back to bed?"

"I don't need to go back to bed," said Mom. "We just need to put on a good show." I could tell by her tone that she was feeling cranky and still a little sick.

I saw Dad standing on the other side of the stage. He waved to me. As I walked over to him, Ruby and Sapphire stopped me. "Your mom is green," said Ruby.

"Not a pretty green," said Sapphire.

"She's fine," I snapped at them. I went to Dad. I was getting really worried. Normally, he would be on the decks supervising the water activities.

"What are you doing here, Dad?" I asked.

"Well, since we can't do any water sports in this weather, I was asked to help out backstage." Dad pulled the big trunk onto the center of the stage.

"Let's get a spotlight right on the trunk," shouted Herby to one of the stagehands. Then he turned to Dad. "Did you hear that your daughter is going to help me out with the magic act?"

"She'll be great," said Dad.

"Okay," said Herby, clapping his hands, "let's get started. Come here, Philippa," he said. "And, Philip, you come out with that beautiful parrot! Now you two will find out why this trunk is so important. It is an exact replica of the last one used by Houdini—the most famous magician of all time! Houdini was the master of the art of making his tricks look so dangerous that the audience was convinced that he would die, and that is what we will do on our stage. I really am an amateur

magician. It's my passion. That's why I always bring that trunk with me. Tonight we will convince our audience that our parrot is truly in peril. I will not only make Don Quixote disappear; I will make him reappear, too."

Don Quixote stared right at me, cocking his head. Philip had once explained to me that parrots had excellent eyesight. They can see more than we can even imagine. I wondered if he could see that I didn't trust Herby.

"Philippa, you and Don Quixote will switch places, like a caterpillar turning into a butterfly, and it will all happen right before the audience's eyes."

"How?" I asked.

"Okay, here's how the trick works," Herby said.

Herby started to fiddle with the bottom of the trunk. He turned it on its side. On the bottom of the trunk was a trapdoor, cleverly disguised so that even when you looked at the trunk closely, you couldn't see it. Herby gave me a long screwdriver, which I was supposed to use to get it open.

"It's easy-peasy," said Herby. "Philip, would it be

possible to take Don Quixote out of his cage? That will make the trick even more dramatic."

"Sure," said Philip. "Don Quixote is fine outside of his cage as long as he is with me or Philippa." Philip opened the door to the birdcage and Don Quixote came out and hopped on his arm. Don Quixote didn't even complain when Philip lowered him into the trunk.

The first time I tried it, I had trouble getting the trapdoor to work. Don Quixote was very patient. I wasn't so patient, but gradually, I learned the trick of getting the trapdoor open.

Philip put Don Quixote into the trunk. Then he and Herby put a curtain around the trunk. I was hidden behind the curtain. It took me a little longer than it should, but I got the trapdoor to work. And I got Don Quixote out.

"Whoo-hoo! It works!" said Herby.

"Whoo-hoo!" repeated Don Quixote on cue. That parrot really was a little ham.

CHAPTER EIGHT

ABRA-CA-COBRA!

Mom had arranged for the costume department to dress Philip and me as pirates. I had a leather corset, a long skirt, big black boots, and a puffy-sleeved shirt. They had made me a lacy pirate hat, and I also had a curved sword that hung from my belt.

Philip was dressed in a black crushed velvet shirt with satin sleeves, and a bandana with a skull print. He refused to wear a pirate hat. He also had big black boots and a leather belt, wrist cuffs, and a matching curved sword that hung from his belt.

I have to admit we looked great. Tonight, Mom's big

pirate extravaganza was going on even if we did have rough seas. All the passengers had been given pirate hats with the ship's logo on it. We peeked through the curtain at the audience. It was a sea of pirates and their "lassies."

"AHOY, MATEYS!" shouted Herby as he bounded onto the stage. He was wearing an elaborate pirate costume, a big puffy shirt with billowing sleeves.

"Whoo-hoo!" Herby sang out. For a tall man, he moved with great grace. His long legs "ate up the floor," which is an expression my mom uses when she sees someone who can really dance.

"What do you get if you cross a magician with a snake?" Herby shouted.

There was a drumroll.

"Abra-ca-*cobra*!" shouted Herby, and then he slipped out a very real-looking snake from his puffy sleeve. This was not something he had done in rehearsal.

I shivered just watching him from backstage. I can dive into the sea without fear. I can climb to the top of the mast on a sailboat and have no fear. But snakes make me shiver. I shrieked.

Philip put his hand over my mouth so the audience wouldn't hear me. "What's wrong?" he whispered.

"The snake," I said, shuddering. "Herby didn't show us the snake in dress rehearsal."

"He did say he had surprises up his sleeve," said Philip.

Don Quixote was bouncing up and down in his cage, shaking a wing and a leg to one side and then the other.

"See? Even Don Quixote is scared," I said to Philip.

"No," said Philip. "Don Quixote is stretching and getting the kinks out of his muscles. He's not scared. You are."

I didn't like having to admit to Philip that he was right. I *was* more scared than his parrot.

Herby came backstage. "You didn't tell me there was going to be a snake in the act," I hissed at him.

"It was just a last-minute addition. One of the passengers gave me the idea, and I remembered I had a rubber snake in my trunk. It *is* just rubber!" said Herby.

"It's very realistic," I said to him.

Don Quixote finished his stretching exercises. I swear he reminded me of Mom when she was about to go on stage.

Herby winked at me. "It's time for a big finale!" He bounded back onto the stage. "And now, ladies and gentlemen, boys and girls," he shouted as he took the stage again. "I bring you, for the first time on any stage, our own captain's son, Philip Vittiganen, and his lovely assistant, Philippa Bath, and the magnificent specimen from Parrot Island, Don Quixote."

And as we walked on stage, as if he knew his cue, Don Quixote squawked out, "FILL UP A BATH!"

Herby had attached a tiny portable microphone to the parrot's cage, so when the sound of Don Quixote's voice went through our state-of-the art sound system, my name came out in surround sound from about one hundred speakers.

The audience howled as if Herby and Don Quixote has just told the best joke in the world.

"Ladies and gentlemen, on this voyage to Parrot Island we have been delayed by Mother Nature, but we are fortunate to have one of the greatest examples of the birds from Parrot Island. May I introduce you to Don Quixote."

Don Quixote bowed his head.

"And tonight—for your amazement—I have a trick that Houdini himself performed. Except Houdini always worked with a human to do this trick. But tonight, Don Quixote will transform himself and change before your very eyes. May I invite someone from the audience to come up and examine the trunk?"

The first one to volunteer was Mrs. Totaa. She was now wearing a bright green boa—it almost matched Don Quixote's feathers. But now she didn't look seasick. She cooed when she saw Don Quixote.

Several other people, all dressed as pirates, clamored to volunteer, including Mr. Papageno. Herby allowed them to examine the trunk. The hinged trapdoor was cleverly hidden because there were so many screws on the bottom. Herby had put sealing wax over the screws. It looked as if it were sealed tight.

The volunteers tipped the trunk on its side, so that the whole audience could see that there was nothing in front of them but an empty trunk.

Philip gently lowered Don Quixote into the trunk and closed the trunk lid. Herby let the audience members stay on stage, while he and Philip pulled a curtain around the trunk.

That was my cue. Herby and Philip's job was to distract the audience with a long joke that Herby had taught him. While Philip was telling the joke, I had to switch places with Don Quixote and put him back in his cage.

"Hey, Philip," said Herby into a microphone. "I've met your parrot. And I know you've got that great long-legged poodle of yours, but do you have any other special pets?"

"Well, Herby," said Philip, "I've got a new pet fish. But to tell the truth, I'm really disappointed in him. The guy who sold him to me said he could sing like a bird."

"What?" asked Herby, doing a double take. "Let me get this straight. You bought a fish because you thought you could teach him to sing like a bird?"

While Herby and Philip were keeping the audience distracted with their silly joke, I got ready to unhinge the trapdoor. Suddenly, I had to stifle a scream. Something slick was around my neck. In the darkness I saw red eyes staring at me, and a gaping mouth full of fangs.

I ran out into the wings. My hands got the tail of the snake. It took me a while to get it unwound from my neck. But it wasn't a snake. It was rubber. It was the rubber snake. What was it doing around my neck?

I flung the snake away. I had lost precious time and I was sweating. I got back to the trunk.

Luckily Herby and Philip were still going on with their joke.

I tipped the trunk on its side, being as silent and gentle as I could. I pulled the cover out of the way and, using the long screwdriver that Herby had given me to unscrew the bottom, I reached in. My hand felt something soft and squishy. It wasn't alive.

It was a stuffed parrot—just like the ones they sell in the gift shop.

I crawled into the trunk. It was empty. No Don Quixote!

Meanwhile, I could hear the audience laughing as Philip and Herby continued their patter.

I tried to scurry around, hoping that somehow in the dark of backstage, Don Quixote was there. Where else could he be? I whistled. No Don Quixote!

On stage Philip was going on with the long fish story unaware that anything was wrong. He was getting close to the punch line. "Well, of course I thought I could teach my fish to sing and to talk, too. He's a parrot fish!" Philip shouted out the words "PARROT FISH!" It was my clue to get into the trunk and get ready. I crawled inside the musty space, still hoping that somehow Don Quixote was in one of its corners. But the trunk was empty.

"Now listen, Philip," said Herby. "I know you're the captain's son and I should be respectful. While you might be able to teach your own parrot to sing, you're never going to get anywhere with a parrot *fish*."

"That's what you think," said Philip, getting into the act. "This fish *can* sing. He just sings terribly off-key. It's driving me crazy. Do you know how hard it is to TUNA FISH?"

That was my cue. When Philip said "tuna fish," I was to be in the trunk ready to pop out!

They pulled the curtain aside.

Herby made a big thing out of unlocking the trunk.

The audience cheered wildly when they saw me instead of Don Quixote. But I wasn't smiling.

Philip grinned. "We did it," he said, squeezing my hand as we took a bow.

"No, we didn't," I whispered as we went backstage.

Philip wasn't listening to me. Herby came backstage and grabbed Philip.

"Come on," he said. "That applause is for you. They want you to come back on stage. You, too, Philippa. And bring Don Quixote."

I shook my head and dug in my heels. I couldn't move. Philip followed Herby back on stage. I could see him taking a bow.

Mom and Dad came up to me. "Sweetheart," Mom said, "go on stage with them. You deserve to take a bow, too. The trick worked wonderfully. I've got to hand it to you. I didn't think Herby could pull it off. The audience loves the act. Philippa, go out there and take your bow."

"Mom, Dad, will you listen to me?" I whispered urgently. "Something is really wrong. Don Quixote is missing!"

CHAPTER NINE

IT'S NOT AN ACT!

Dad sprung into action. He got all the stagehands to help. We scoured through all the props backstage. There were so many places that a parrot could perch or try to hide.

We looked high and low, and we couldn't find a sign of him. Not even a feather.

"What's wrong?" asked Herby, when he came backstage followed by Philip. "Why didn't you come out for the bow? They want to see the parrot and you! It's part of the act."

"It's not an act!" I shouted at him. "Don Quixote never came out of the trunk!"

"What? How can that be?" exclaimed Herby. "In rehearsal the trick worked perfectly!"

Philip was looking at me, as if he were in shock. I knew how much Don Quixote meant to him. Don Quixote, like Max, his great poodle, was one of the only living ties to his mother.

"What happened?" asked Philip in a voice so quiet and calm it sounded almost deadly.

"Someone got me out of the way by putting a snake around my neck. It was a fake snake, but I didn't know that. I ran. By the time I got back and I opened the trapdoor, Don Quixote had disappeared and in his place was a stuffed parrot."

"Impossible!" said Herby.

I glared at him. "It happened! I'm not making it up!"

Just then the captain came backstage, followed by Camilla. "Mr. Twining, Philip, Philippa," the captain said, "I have to congratulate you. You put on a wonderful show. The audience loved it. Didn't they, Camilla?"

Camilla looked as if she had just swallowed a rotten oyster. "I have to say, it *was* amusing. You tied in the

Parrot and Pirate theme very nicely. All in all, it went rather well."

"It didn't go well at all!" I shouted. "It was a disaster. Don Quixote is missing."

"What?" exclaimed the captain.

I wanted to disappear into Houdini's box myself. You never want to get the captain angry.

"Where is Don Quixote?" the captain demanded.

"I don't know," said Herby. "Philippa was backstage. She was supposed to get him out of the trunk."

I hated Herby for blaming me, even if he was telling the truth.

"I'm so sorry, Captain," I mumbled. "I don't know what happened. Somebody deliberately used that rubber snake to get me away from the box. It had to be someone who knew I was scared of snakes. I was so scared that I ran halfway across the room and I was gone probably about a minute or two—long enough for someone to take Don Quixote." I felt close to tears. The more I talked the more responsible I felt for Don Quixote's disappearance.

"I didn't know you were afraid of snakes," said Herby.

I shot him a suspicious look. Before I could say anything, Dad came up to us. He looked grimy and full of
dirt. "We've been searching the whole backstage for
him," said Dad. "We can't find the parrot."

Captain Vittiganen put his hand gently on Philip's
shoulder. "Don Quixote is a beloved member of my
family," he said softly. "He was my late wife's pet. She
had him ever since she was a child, and since she died,
Don Quixote has lived with my son and me."

"Father," pleaded Philip, "you must get the entire
crew to search the ship. We have to find him."

The captain sighed. "Philip, I really can't spare any
more of my crew right now. We are now sailing back on
course for Parrot Island, and we are trying to make up
for lost time."

"But, Father! We have to find Don Quixote now!
We must!"

"I know, I know," said Captain Vittiganen, sounding
upset. "But we have to look at the bright side. That bird
has survived revolutions and shipwrecks, and he's had
more adventures than a cat with nine lives. Maybe he
is playing a game of hide-and-seek. Philippa let him out

of her sight for a moment, but it's not really her fault. I'm sure he will be found."

The captain sounded hopeful. But Philip didn't look as if he were buying it.

"Yes, Don Quixote likes to play hide-and-seek," said Philip. "But that is in our quarters. He would never do it in a strange place."

The captain hugged his son. "Philip, I am sure that Don Quixote will be found. It has only been a few minutes. Do not worry."

Philip wouldn't look at me. I couldn't believe that everything had gone so horribly wrong so quickly.

"We'll find him, sir," said Herby.

I glared at him. It was all Herby Twining's fault. If he hadn't taken over the pirate night with his stupid magic trick, none of this would have happened.

CHAPTER TEN

THREE OF THE SCARIEST WORDS: LEAVE ME ALONE!

I was feeling desperate. "Philip," I said, "didn't you tell me that parrots are very loyal? Maybe Don Quixote made his way back up to your stateroom. Let's go look."

"My stateroom is five stories above the theater. What do you think he did? Take the elevator?"

"Parrots can fly," I said. "He could be there."

Philip sighed. "Have you really looked all over backstage?"

"We did," said my dad. "We couldn't find him anywhere."

Philip's shoulders slumped.

"Okay," he said. "I guess it's worth a try."

"We'll keep looking for him here," my father promised Philip.

On our way to Philip's stateroom, we ran into Mr. Papageno carrying his suitcase full of artist's materials. "Wonderful show. Wonderful show, you two," he said. "Most entertaining..."

We really didn't have time for him right now.

"I still want to paint you two," said Mr. Papageno.

"Not now," I said as politely as I could. I needed to talk to Philip alone and soon!

We opened the door to Philip's stateroom. The mechanical birds that had once frightened me sat silently on their perches. But there was no live parrot anywhere. I hadn't really believed that he would be there. I had just wanted to talk to Philip alone. I put my hand on Philip's shoulder.

He jumped. He seemed as jumpy as a kitten. "I should never have let Don Quixote be in the magic show. It's my fault."

"It is not your fault!" I said to him.

"Yes, it is my fault," said Philip. "I think all that noise frightened him, and he flew off. It was me who let him out of the cage to put him in the trunk. And now he could be anywhere."

"He didn't fly off and he didn't leave you!" I insisted. "It was a carefully planned parrot snatching. Don Quixote is one of the most valuable parrots in the world. I told you that pirates used to steal parrots so they could sell them, right? Well, I think we have a pirate on board. He's been planning on stealing Don Quixote from the beginning…"

"And I suppose you've solved this mystery on your own," said Philip sarcastically.

"I did," I said. "It is Herby 'Whoo-hoo' Twining… And I can prove it," I insisted. "I've got a list in my head."

I sat down at Philip's computer. Philip looked over my shoulder as I hit the keyboard and put in my bullet points:

- Herby wasn't hired the normal way.
  Why did they send a pilot boat for him?
  I think he paid someone to get him a job
  on board our ship.

- Herby brought a trunk with him. Nobody who works on a crew comes with that much luggage. So he was planning on doing that magic trick from the beginning in order to steal Don Quixote.
- He doesn't know anything about how a crewmember would behave on a cruise ship. He didn't know that most of the crew sleeps below the waterline.
- He insulted Camilla with his Trout dance. NOBODY who had ever worked on a cruise ship would make fun of the cruise director in public!
- He was the one who talked us into using the parrot for his magic show.
- The snake! He said that he didn't know I was afraid of snakes. But he did. He was there when I first saw Mr. Papageno's creepy necklace. You told everyone that I was afraid of snakes.
- That's why Herby used a snake in the final act without telling us. He wanted to get me distracted.

- Herby is the one who knows best how to use the trapdoor in the trunk. He stole Don Quixote and hid him somewhere.
- Maybe he had an accomplice. You, Philip, gave me the clue. Mrs. Totaa's name even means bird. She's always wearing a boa. Boas are like snakes. She could be working with Herby. Maybe the boa is secretly a trap to capture parrots . . . She was the first one to volunteer.

I stopped typing. I took a deep breath and looked up. "Okay, maybe that last one is a bit of a stretch, but what do you think?" I let him read over my shoulder what I had been writing on the screen.

Philip wouldn't look at me. He looked out his window at the balcony, as if he were willing Don Quixote to make an appearance. "It doesn't add up," he mumbled.

"My list is scientific," I argued. "It proves that Herby is behind Don Quixote's disappearance. You and I— we solve mysteries together. Remember the first time we met? We both said that we love mysteries."

"I remember, Philippa," said Philip, but he was using his cold "royal" voice. "I also remember that you've seemed to have it in for Herby from the first day you met him. You are almost worse than Camilla."

I felt as if Philip had slapped me across the face.

"That's so unfair," I protested. "Philip, you know I think logically. I thought this through. I know it was Herby. All right, maybe at first, I thought he was sent from the cruise line to make cuts in the crew. I even thought maybe he was plotting against you because you were from Borgunlund. I was wrong about that. I think he came deliberately because he wanted to take your parrot."

Philip punched the print button on his computer and then picked up my list and started picking it apart:

"Number one: Herby wasn't hired in the normal way. Well, so what? We get hires all the time from somebody who knows somebody in the cruise line. And he happens to be very good at what he does.

"Number two: Herby came on with the trunk because he is a MAGICIAN! And a good one!

"Number three: He doesn't act as if he's been on a

cruise ship before. Well, maybe he worked on one of those very small cruise boats with fewer passengers.

"Number four: He thought of using Don Quixote in the magic act. It was pirate night! You were the one who told me that parrots and pirates go together. It was natural that he would think of using Don Quixote in the act.

"Number five: The snake was funny. Everybody but you could tell it was a make-believe snake. You just happen to be very gullible when it comes to snakes.

"Number six: Mrs. Totaa is a harmless bird-watcher. She can barely keep her binoculars and her boa around her neck. She certainly wouldn't have been able to sneak backstage and put a rubber snake around you."

Philip started to laugh. "Or are you going to tell me that you're scared of feather boas as much as you are scared of snakes. Because if she had put anything around your neck it would have been one of her boas."

Philip paused.

I jumped on his pause. "Philip Vittiganen, don't you believe anything I am telling you?"

"Well, look at your list," said Philip, shaking it at me. "Your list just shows me that you are being as judgmental as Camilla. And even she changed her mind about Herby. Even she and Ruby and Sapphire are nicer to Herby than you are. They give him the benefit of the doubt. But you've had it in for him from the beginning."

"How dare you compare me to Ruby and Sapphire."

"I said they were nicer to Herby than you are!" I yelled. "Maybe you don't think *I'm* a nice person."

Philip looked at me coldly. I guess nobody is supposed to yell at the Royal Prince of Borgunlund.

"Philippa," said Philip in his coldest voice. "Please, leave me alone right now."

"Okay, I will leave you alone," I said. "I'll find Don Quixote myself. I'll solve the mystery of his disappearance *by myself.*"

I slammed the door as I left the captain's quarters. I was never going to let him see me cry. But I was crying. I couldn't help it. I bawled my eyes out.

CHAPTER ELEVEN

80 PERCENT WATER

The next morning, I went to the room where Captain Raynor tutors Philip, Sapphire, Ruby, and me. Captain Raynor is our retired captain, but he stays on the ship, and he is our teacher—we are all 'ship-schooled.'

For our tutoring sessions, usually Philip and I sit together, but today, we sat with our backs to each other without saying a word.

"Did you know that the human body is made up of 80 percent water?" asked Captain Raynor. "It's why I think we are so affected by the tides and the full moon. Scientists believe that humans are affected by the pull of the moon, the same way that the sea is."

"That's silly," said Ruby.

"Yeah, silly," repeated Sapphire.

Normally, that would be the cue for Philip and me to look at each other and roll our eyes. But Philip and I both remained silent.

Captain Raynor sighed. "Maybe the full moon has something to do with the tension in the room today," he said under his breath.

I snuck a glance at Philip. He wouldn't look at me. Okay, if he wouldn't look at me, I wouldn't look at him.

"Let's leave science for the moment," said Captain Raynor. "Let's review our Latin." Captain Raynor loves Latin. He says that even if the Romans are long dead and nobody speaks Latin anymore, that you can understand what words really mean if you learn Latin.

"Does anyone remember what the prefix *ex-* means?" asked Captain Raynor.

"It comes from the Latin to mean *out*," said Philip. "*Exit* combines the Latin word *ire*—to *go*, as in 'Get out!'"

"Or *ex*-friends," I muttered under my breath.

Captain Raynor sighed. "Let's take out our work-sheets and write down all the '*Ex*-amples,' of words that start with the Latin prefix *ex-*. By the way, *Example* is a Latin word that comes from *exemplum*..."

Captain Raynor handed out worksheets. Philip always got 100 on the Latin tests because he already spoke so many languages.

"I'll put on a little Mozart for some *ex*-hilaration," said Captain Raynor, "while you do your worksheets."

Captain Raynor loves opera, and he often puts it on when we are working. I think he believes that Mozart is the cure for everything! But I knew that Mozart wasn't going to cure my problems.

"I think that today we could all use a little exhilaration," said Captain Raynor. "It comes from the Latin word *hilarare*, which means 'to gladden,' when something is hilarious."

"I've got a hilarious joke!" said Ruby. "Knock-knock."

"Knock-knock," repeated Sapphire.

"You're supposed to say 'who's there,'" I reminded her. I looked at Philip. Normally we would have laughed together about the Trout twins repeating each other so much that they couldn't even tell a knock-knock joke straight.

"Who's there?" answered Sapphire.

"Latin," said Ruby.

"Latin who?" asked Sapphire.

"Latin me in, please. I've been knocking on your door for a long time."

Philip laughed. I sighed. It had come to this. Philip was laughing at Ruby and Sapphire's jokes. I started to well up again.

Captain Raynor looked at me. "Is something wrong?" he whispered to me.

I shook my head. "No," I mumbled. "The music is so beautiful it makes me cry."

Captain Raynor nodded. He collected our papers. Mine was blotched with tearstains. "Why don't we take a break?" he said.

Philip exited the room like a lightning bolt, as if he couldn't wait to get away from me. Ruby and Sapphire ran after him. I knew they were happy that Philip and I weren't speaking. The twins have always been jealous that the captain's son is my friend and not theirs.

I started to get up. "Philippa," said Captain Raynor, "what's wrong?" he asked.

"*Nusquam,*" I answered him, using the Latin word for "nothing."

"It's not nothing," said Captain Raynor. "What's going on with you and Philip?"

"Nothing," I repeated.

"You and Philip both sit in my class as if you are somewhere else. You aren't talking to each other. This is not *nusquam* or nothing."

I listened to the music. It had changed into something that sounded very silly, but even though it was silly I still couldn't stop crying.

"It's just that the music is so beautiful," I lied.

"Very few people cry at Papageno's song. It was Mozart's chance to be silly. Mozart had a great sense of humor . . . and this is one of his funniest operas."

"Whose song?" I asked

"Papageno," said Captain Raynor.

I sat up a little straighter. Finally my tear ducts stopped leaking and the gears in my brain started to turn.

It's hard to think like a detective when you're crying. "What does *Papageno* mean?" I asked.

"He's the bird catcher," said Captain Raynor. "He's a very funny character, and he loves to tell lies and tall tales. In fact, I must make a note to teach the *Magic Flute*. It is a wonderful opera for children."

"And there's a character in it who's a bird catcher," I said.

"Yes…and he dresses up as a bird. He's a very funny…" Captain Raynor began to chuckle.

I didn't.

I jumped up. "Thank you, Captain Raynor." I gave him a kiss. The fact that *Papageno* meant bird catcher had to be a clue. Herby hadn't been working alone. He had an accomplice. Maybe I *had* been wrong, and it hadn't been Mrs. Totaa. But it could be Mr. Papageno. This shed a whole new light on everything. If it was Mr. Pappegno, then he could have hidden Don Quixote in the suitcase that he claimed was full of art supplies. More than anything, I wanted to talk it over with Philip.

I went to the captain's quarters and knocked on the door.

There was no answer.

"Knock! Knock!" I shouted. No one answered.

If Philip was in his room, he wasn't coming out for me. Finally the captain came walking down the hallway. He saw me slumped down in the corridor in front of his stateroom.

"Philippa," he said rather gently. "What are you doing here?"

"I wanted to talk to Philip," I said.

"He's resting," said the captain. I looked at my watch. It was only four in the afternoon. Philip never took a nap.

"You mean, he doesn't want to see me," I said.

"He's upset right now about Don Quixote. Perhaps I never should have agreed to sail to Parrot Island." Captain Vittiganen sighed. "It brings back so many bad memories . . ."

"I know it's where your wife died," I said. "I'm so sorry it has such sad memories."

"But it has joyful memories, too," said the captain. "That's why Philip and I decided that we would go there together. And he wanted to show it to you." The captain paused. "Give Philip some time," he said.

I wondered how much Philip had told his father about our fight. I felt close to tears again. If our bodies were 80 percent water, I had cried so much lately that I must have been causing a drought in my own body.

CHAPTER TWELVE
THINK OUTSIDE THE BOX

I didn't sleep well that night. I looked at the digital clock next to my bed. It was only five o'clock in the morning, but I couldn't stay in bed any longer.

I got up quietly and let myself out onto the decks. I went to the kennel. Max wagged his tail when he saw me. "Hi, boy," I said to him sadly. "Your owner and I aren't getting along right now." Max didn't seem to care. He wagged his tail even harder. I swallowed hard. What would it be like if Philip and I stopped being friends, never had our walks on deck with our dogs when we talked everything over?

At least Lady Windermere was happy to see me. I picked her up, hugged her tight and snapped her leash on.

The sea always calms me. I love it. The crash of the bow through the waves was loud yet soothing, much like the surf crashing against a shore. At this hour, just before dawn, it was mostly dark and the full moon was about to slip under the horizon. I wondered if the tides were pulling at my body—maybe that's why I felt so pulled apart.

Seagulls screeched overhead, a sure sign that we were nearing land—Parrot Island.

I had been so excited to go to Parrot Island with Philip. But now I felt as if those dreams were like ashes from the volcano that loomed over Parrot Island. Okay, I was being melodramatic, but really:

- Don Quixote had not been found.
- Philip and I were not talking.

This was the worst voyage of my life.

I didn't realize how long I had been standing there with Lady Windermere, staring out to sea. My father came up to me on the deck. "I was looking for you. I heard you leave our room before dawn. Are you okay?"

"Not really." I shrugged. "How's Mom? Is she all over being seasick?"

"She's feeling fine," he said. "It's you we're worried about." He kissed me on the top of the head. "You seem so sad. Will you talk to me about it? I know you and Philip are upset about Don Quixote."

"It's not just that," I said. "We had a big fight."

"Friends fight all the time, and then make up. The two of you have a very special friendship."

"Not anymore, we don't," I said. I started to sniffle again. "He's a jerk! A total and absolute jerk."

My father was smart enough not to say anything.

"I hate him," I said. "I absolutely hate him." But as soon as I said that word *hate*, the tears started gushing even though I didn't want them to.

"You don't hate him," said Dad. "Honey, you're very angry right now, but you know that Philip is your friend. You're just worried because Don Quixote hasn't been found."

"But Philip doesn't trust me to help him find him . . .

and we always solve mysteries together. But how can we work together if he doesn't trust me?"

"Philippa," said Dad. "You know Philip grew up in a world where he was taught not to trust anybody."

"Dad, I don't think Herby Twining can be trusted. It's as if I've got the pieces, but I can't quite fit them together. Maybe it's because Philip isn't helping me. At first I thought maybe Herby is a spy from the cruise line and he wants to get you and Mom fired and kick Lady Windermere and me off the boat."

Dad looked at me. "Philippa," he said, "What are you talking about?"

"I heard that the cruise line is looking to make cuts, and maybe Herby came on board to see if they can cut you and Mom."

"I think you're barking up the wrong tree with that one," said Dad.

"I'm not," I insisted.

My dad put his hands on either side of my cheeks. "Philippa, look at me. Nobody is going to get us fired. We have a contract with the cruise line. In fact, we were just offered another contract for two more years.

One of the reasons we were so glad to get the new contract was that we didn't want to separate you from Philip. You two are good for each other. You study well together. Your mom and I feel that you are having much more fun on the ship now that Philip is here. The captain told us that he feels the same way. He's very grateful for your friendship with Philip. He told us that before Philip met you, there were very few people his own age that he connected with. We were worried you didn't have someone your age on ship that you could be friends with. And then you found Philip. You both love adventures, and you are becoming loyal friends. That's something too valuable to lose just because of a stupid fight."

"Dad," I said. "It doesn't feel like a stupid fight. I went to talk to him, and he's practically locked up in his room and won't come out."

"You know that Philip has very sad memories of Parrot Island. And now his beloved parrot is missing. He needs your help. This is one time where you have to be the bigger person."

"I'm not that big," I mumbled.

"Yes, you are," said Dad, kissing me again on the top

of the head. "Life's not always a picnic . . . but you're big enough to help your friend."

"But I don't know how," I said. "I don't have the foggiest idea where Don Quixote is."

"Think outside the box," said Dad.

My mouth dropped open. "The box," I mumbled. "The secret has to be *inside* the box."

Dad looked at me as if I had turned into a loony bird. But I hadn't. I had an idea now of how Mr. Papageno and Herby had managed to steal Don Quixote. There were boxes inside boxes! He had help. Now all I had to do was prove it!

CHAPTER THIRTEEN

THE PARROT PIRATE

As we got closer to Parrot Island the weather cleared up. The sky was the color of a robin's egg, and all signs of the storm seemed to have disappeared. The air after a storm is always that much sweeter because of the soft winds that blow, making everything seem fresh.

I felt much fresher, too. Dad had said to think outside of the box, and I was pretty sure that the clue to Don Quixote's disappearance had to be inside Houdini's magic trunk. Where there was one trapdoor, there had to be another.

I went to the backstage area of the theater. I ran into

one of the stagehands. "Hi," I said. "Herby Twining asked me to get something that he left in the trunk we were using for the magic show. He's going on Parrot Island with a tour and he forgot something."

The stagehand knew me well and, of course, he knew that Herby had used me as his magician's assistant. He let me into the backstage area without any hesitation.

The box was still standing in the middle of the stage. I told myself to focus. When we did the magic trick, there had to be another trapdoor in the trunk where they had hidden Don Quixote. Perhaps the bottom of the trunk had mirrors in it.

I examined the box from the inside out. I kept tapping at it. I knew there had to be a secret hinge somewhere. Then I looked closely.

I saw the tracks of wheels in the dust.

Suddenly, I felt someone tap my shoulder. "Whoohoo!" It was Herby.

I stood up, trying to make myself as tall as I could. It was now or never. I had to confront Herby if I was going to get the truth. "Herby Twining," I said, "I know that somehow you took Don Quixote, and I'm not leaving

until I find out how. I'm pretty sure that Mr. Papageno or maybe Mrs. Totaa helped you get Don Quixote out while you distracted me with that fake snake!"

"Philippa, you are barking up the wrong tree," said Herby. "I am on your side."

"WOOF! WOOF!" I barked back at him. "Dad said I was barking up the wrong tree, too. But I know I'm right! You somehow took Don Quixote, and I am going to prove it." I kept tapping at the box.

Herby reached into his pocket. I thought he was going to take out another buzzer ... except maybe this time it would give me a real shock, but he pulled out a piece of paper.

He handed it to me.

"Read it," he said.

It was from the head of the cruise line, explaining that Herby Twining was an environmental detective, who had gotten wind of a plot to exploit the endangered species of parrots on Parrot Island. I squinted at it.

"Is this for real?" I asked him.

Herby nodded. "The head of the cruise line is a major supporter of environmental protection. We heard rumors that there was going to be a smuggling operation out of Parrot Island to capture the birds. So we hoped to set a trap. I was sent aboard to investigate who was doing the smuggling. And by the way, I really am an amateur magician. Okay, maybe I overdid the goofy part—but I thought that would make me more believable as an assistant cruise director."

"You were a very believable goof-ball," I told him.

"Thank you," said Herby. "It comes naturally to me. I thought that if we did the parrot act, I would flush out the pirates who were overly interested in parrots. But I never dreamed that they would take the parrot already on board. I need to ask you again. At the moment Don Quixote disappeared, you said that someone put my fake snake around your neck. Then what happened? Maybe in the search for Don Quixote, I missed a clue. I thought you had just messed up the trick a little."

"I did."

"When the snake went around your neck, were you distracted long enough so that someone could get to the trunk?"

I nodded.

"Well then, I think it's probably a case of the parrot pirate. The guy's been stealing rare birds for a decade."

"The parrot pirate?" I asked Herby.

Herby sighed. "I came on board to protect the parrots of Parrot Island. I never dreamed that Don Quixote would be in danger. But I was stupid. I want us to work together."

"So you aren't working with Mr. Papageno or Mrs. Totaa?"

"No," said Herby. "Who's Mrs. Totaa? Who's Mr. Papageno?"

I thought for a moment. "Mr. Papageno! He had a rattlesnake's tooth around his neck, and he saw that it creeped me out."

"Philippa," said Herby. "Who are these people— Mr. Papageno? Mrs. Totaa?"

I stared at him. "Mrs. Totaa wears a boa all the time and Mr. Papageno is the man who goes around with his art supplies in his suitcase."

"There are so many passengers that I can't tell them apart. And they are all dressed up as pirates!"

That's when I knew that Herby was telling the truth.

He really wasn't someone who had ever worked on a cruise line before. My mom and dad, and everyone who works with the customers, are trained to memorize passengers' names. It makes the passengers feel good because they love to think that they are memorable. Even I have gotten good at remembering passengers' names.

"*Totaa* means 'bird' in Hindi. I just found out that *Papageno* means 'parrot catcher.' It comes from a Mozart opera."

Herby shook his head. "I guess I should have stayed awake during my classical musical appreciation course at college," he said.

Herby examined the trunk. "Do you see those wheel marks?" he asked. "They look like they came from a big suitcase. Which one of them has the suitcase?"

"Mr. Papageno, "I said.

"Now, I remember," said Herby. "It was he who gave me the rubber snake. He said it would be a funny addition."

"Wow, Captain Raynor is right. It pays to listen to Mozart after all."

Herby was down on all fours looking at the trunk.

"These wheel marks were not here when we were rehearsing," said Herby. "I bet that's how he got the parrot away from here," said Herby, jumping up. "I'm sure he's hoping to find a mate for Don Quixote and breed them, which is completely against the law. We've got to catch him. Come with me. I'm going to tell the captain to stop him from leaving the ship."

CHAPTER FOURTEEN
ROMANCE ON PARROT ISLAND

Parrot Island was so small that we couldn't pull the cruise ship directly to the island. We anchored outside the harbor, and then passengers were ferried to the dock.

We ran up to the captain. He was overseeing the transfer to the excursions on Parrot Island.

I saw Mr. Papageno wheeling his big suitcase onto one of the transport boats. He got on it before we could stop him. Mrs. Totaa was on the next to last boat. She waved the end of her boa at me as she got on.

Herby explained to the captain that he believed that Mr. Papageno was behind the disappearance, and that he was the 'person of interest' they had suspected of exploiting the endangered parrots of Parrot Island.

"I'm going after him," said Herby.

"Philip should be with you," I said. "If Mr. Papageno has Don Quixote, Philip might be the only one who can calm the parrot down."

"Good idea," said Herby. "Philippa, will you go get him?"

I looked at the captain, and he nodded. Philip was several feet away, leaning on the railing of the deck, looking out at Parrot Island.

I went over to him.

"You were right about Herby," I said quietly. "He isn't the bad guy."

Philip wouldn't look at me.

I sighed. I could see from the side that his eyes were watery.

"I'm not the bad guy, either," I said. "I made a mistake, but that doesn't mean I'm not still your friend. Herby and I think we know how to find Don Quixote and you should come with us."

Philip turned to me. He mumbled something.

"I couldn't hear you," I said.

He sniffled. "I hated being mad at you," he said. "I just didn't know what to believe. I knew you didn't like Herby as much as I did, and then when I lost Don Quixote, I felt lost."

"Listen," I said, "We've both cried enough lately to fill up an ocean. You and I have to pull together . . . and we'll find Don Quixote."

"But you seemed so angry," said Philip softly. "And I got angry too."

"Philip," I said, grabbing him, "Real friends say lots of stuff. Do you want Don Quixote back or not?"

Herby ran up to Philip and me. "Philippa, I've asked your father to take one of the transport boats. He's willing to go on the search with us."

"Come on," I said to Philip. I grabbed his hand. It felt warm.

"Let's go!" I shouted to Dad, as we jumped onto the cigarette boat, the fastest transport boat that we had.

The wind whipped my hair into my eyes. Herby and Dad were in the front of the boat.

"Papageno was on the first transport boat," Herby

explained to my father. "Do you know where they're taking them?"

"They take them on an excursion of Macaw Cove," said Dad. "There are boardwalks around the nesting ground so that the passengers can get close to the parrots without disturbing their nests."

Herby nodded. "My guess is that if those pirates wanted to go 'rogue' and try to capture a parrot on their own, they'd go there first. In the wild, parrots tend to live in flocks," said Herby. "That's why they make such good pets. They are very sociable creatures. The parrots of Parrot Island are very tame. Because it is a nature preserve, they have no natural predators. But today these parrots have a good reason to be afraid."

"Then we better get there before them," said Dad. He gunned the engine.

"Are you okay?" I shouted to Philip. He was being awfully quiet as we sped across the beautiful cove.

Philip shook his head. "This is the cove where my mother met her accident." He gave me a smile. "I was just thinking how happy my mother would be that I was going to rescue Don Quixote with my friend."

I nodded.

"It will all be worth it to come back here if we can get Don Quixote back," said Philip.

"We will," I promised him.

Dad put up his hand. "Look," he said. He took out his binoculars.

"There's another boat waiting in the marshes over there. It's not one of ours."

"My guess is that it is the real accomplice of Mr. Papageno," said Herby. He got out his own binoculars. "It's not your lady with the boa."

"I can see the tour," continued Herby. "There's a guy wheeling a suitcase. Is that him?"

Herby gave the binoculars to me. His binoculars were the most powerful ones I had ever used. It was as if Mr. Papageno was standing right next to me. I could see the rattlesnake's tooth dangling from his neck.

"That's him," I said.

Dad knew the coves of Parrot Island as well as anyone. He turned off the engine and let the boat drift into a hidden cove. He maneuvered us so we were just a few feet from the boardwalk and yet hidden from view of the outlaw boat.

We watched as Mr. Papageno pretended to stumble.

"You go on," he said to the tour director. His voice carried over the water. "I think I twisted my ankle. You can pick me up when you're finished."

Mr. Papageno let the rest of the tour get ahead of him. A parrot perched on one of the trees near him.

"It's a female," Philip whispered to me.

"How can you tell?" I asked.

"She's got a slender neck and a smaller head than Don Quixote. And she doesn't have the red wing tip that Don Quixote has."

We watched as Mr. Papageno reached into the outer pocket of his suitcase and pulled out a collapsible net.

Herby and my father inched closer, warning Philip and me to stay back.

With a practiced move, Mr. Papageno grabbed the female parrot. We could barely hear the squawk, before he put a bag over her head, and quickly opened his suitcase and stuffed her inside.

Then he signaled to the man in the hidden cove to

come closer. That's how he was going to do it! He was going to give his accomplice the endangered female parrot and Don Quixote. Then he thought he could continue with the cruise without anyone suspecting.

Dad and Herby jumped from the bushes and tackled him. Mr. Papageno's accomplice saw what was happening and gunned his boat's motor and took off.

"What are you doing here?" Mr. Papageno shouted as Dad and Herby grabbed him by the arms.

"Arresting you for trafficking in endangered species," said Herby, whipping out his handcuffs.

Meanwhile, Dad went to the suitcase. The sides of the suitcase were heaving.

"Let's go," I said to Philip.

"They told us to wait here," Philip said.

"Come on, Philip," I urged. "Mr. Papageno is handcuffed. The other boat sped away. Don't you want to be the first one who Don Quixote sees?"

"Do you really think he is safe inside that suitcase?" Philip asked. He sounded worried.

"Well, who better than us to find out!" I shouted. "Come on!"

Philip scrambled out of the boat with me.

We got to Dad just as he wrestled the suitcase open.

The parrot that had just been captured came out flying! She flapped her wings angrily and flew to a tree and started squawking her head off.

Then Dad signaled for Philip to come forward. In a compartment in the suitcase with airholes in the side, there was Don Quixote, looking very unhappy.

"You're safe . . . you're safe!" I said overjoyed. I helped Philip release Don Quixote from that horrible cell of a suitcase. He perched on Philip's arm the way he had been trained. Just to be safe, I took one of the straps from the suitcase, and put it around Don Quixote's leg. He didn't even peck me. He just nodded his beautiful head. I stroked his feathers.

"Is he all right?" Herby asked.

"He seems fine," said Philip.

"You were planning on breeding a pair, weren't you?" demanded Herby, getting his face into Mr. Papageno's.

"His offspring would have fetched a fortune," snarled Mr. Papageno.

"A fortune you'll never see in jail," said Herby. He

turned to us. "Once we get to a major port I'll take him to the authorities. Right now I have to make sure that all the paperwork is correct."

Dad shook Herby's hand. "You know," said Dad, "I'd like to have a rematch on our Ping-Pong game sometime."

Herby grinned. "Me, too."

Herby came over to Philip and me. "I need to thank you both. I would have completely botched up this job if it weren't for you."

"Thanks to Philippa," said Philip. "She was the one who figured it out."

"No, I didn't," I said. "Not by myself. If we hadn't had that fight, I would never have started crying to Mozart, and Mr. Papageno might have gotten away with it."

Mr. Papageno heard me. "That name was my little joke," said Mr. Papageno. "I knew the authorities would be too stupid to figure it out."

"We're not that stupid," snapped Herby. "We'll find out your real name. We see this a lot with creeps like you who go after rare animals. You get a kick out of thinking we're stupid."

"He even told a million parrot jokes," I said.

"He fooled me," said Herby. "But he didn't fool you. You can spend your time in jail figuring out how a little girl was the one who was able to catch you in the act."

"I'm not a little girl," I protested.

"I didn't mean it as an insult," said Herby. "Shake."

He held out his hand. Of course I got buzzed.

Philip laughed.

"Herby," said Dad. "You were pretty good as an assistant cruise director. Maybe you should think of a change in careers."

Herby grinned at us again. "You know, in college I was an entertainer. I starred in all our shows. And I do love magic. Maybe I will consider a change of careers." He marched Mr. Papageno off, and then turned back to us. "Whoo-hoo!" he shouted.

Don Quixote perched on Philip's arm and lifted his great head up to the sky. He made a trilling noise that seemed to come from the back of the throat. It was a sound that I had never heard.

Up on the tree, we heard the same trilling noise. The group of bird watchers from the ship were walking along the boardwalk coming closer. Mrs. Totaa was in the lead.

"What's happening?" she asked.

"Don Quixote has been found," I said. "And Mr. Papegeno has been arrested."

"You know, I became a bird-watcher because my name made me always relate to birds, but I wondered about Mr. Papegeno. He seemed a little bit odd. He always talked about painting birds, but I never saw him painting. It felt like an odd coincidence that both our names were related to birds."

"I don't think Papegeno is his real name," I said. "He was known as the Parrot Pirate."

"Listen," said Mrs. Totaa. She cocked her head and looked a little like Don Quixote. She looked up at the tree. "That's the female of the species. That's the sound they make when they're in heat. How thrilling!"

Philip blushed.

"What does that mean?" I asked him.

"That's the sound that parrots in the wild make when they're courting."

I stared at Don Quixote. Then I smiled. "Maybe when we come back next year, there will be little Don Quixotes."

"Fill up a bath!" Don Quixote squawked.

"Okay, sir," I said to him. "You're the boss."

Philip smiled at me. "He really is bossy, isn't he? But from now on, I will help you clean his cage. We will do it together."

"Whoo-hoo!" squawked Don Quixote.